This book belongs to

....

Tips for the Storyteller

Don't Rock the Boat! is an amusing story about a bunch of funny animals. It will make children laugh – and also encourage them to count. Children will love looking at the pictures, joining in with the text, and guessing what will happen at the end.

Keep reading to find out how to get the most fun out of this story.

Read and count

This story combines reading, counting, and fun. Read it straight through the first time so your child will enjoy the joke. As you read it for a second time, encourage your child to count the animals with you. At the end of the story, you could also count the presents and the animals' party hats.

3 puppies

Animal talk

At the end of the story, Dottie the Donkey says, *"Hee-haw! Hee-haw!"* Point to the other animals in the story and talk to your child about the noises they make. Ask him which animal noise he likes best. Your child will enjoy making the noises with you as you read the story.

Hee-haw! Hee-haw!

Oink! Oink!

Hee-haw!

Oink! Oink.

Don't rock the boat!

Enjoy the repetition

There are lots of repeated phrases that give this story a memorable rhythm and pattern. Once you have read the story a few times, your child will love joining in. Let her call out, "Can we come with you?", wait for her to name the animals that come next, and encourage her to shout out, "Don't rock the boat!" Saying the repeated phrases, following the words, and turning the pages will increase your child's enjoyment of the story and make her more confident about reading.

Story clues

Looking at the pictures and predicting what will happen is an important reading skill to develop. Before you or your child turn the page, look at the pictures and ask your child if he thinks the animals are going to rock the boat. Can he guess what might happen if the animals do rock the boat?

Have a good time counting and enjoy the story!

For my father, Peter W. Battle - Sarah Battle

LONDON, NEW YORK, SYDNEY, DELHI, PARIS,
MUNICH, and JOHANNESBURG

First American Edition, 2001
Published in the United States by
DK Publishing, Inc.
95 Madison Avenue
New York, New York 10016

01 02 03 04 05 10 9 8 7 6 5 4 3 2 1

Library of Congress Cataloging-in-Publication Data
Grindley, Sally
Don't rock the boat / by Sally Grindley ; illustrated by Sarah Battle. - 1st American ed.
p. cm. - (Share-a-story)
Summary: A group of animal friends share a boat ride so that they will keep nice and clean on their way to Grey Donkey's party.
ISBN 0-7894-7892-7 - ISBN 0-7894-7893-5 (pbk.)
[I. Boats and boating - Fiction. 2. Animals - Fiction.] I. Battle, Sarah, ill. II. Title. III. Share-a-story (DK Publishing, Inc.)
PZ7. G88446 Do 2001   [E] - dc21   2001028507

Color reproduction by Dot Gradations, UK
Printed in Hong Kong by Wing King Tong

Acknowledgments:
Series Reading Consultant: Wendy Cooling   **Activities Advisor:** Dawn Sirett
Photographer: Zara Ronchi   **Models:** Hannah Shone, Cal Stuart, and Juliett Preston

see our complete
catalog at
www.dk.com

Don't Rock the Boat!

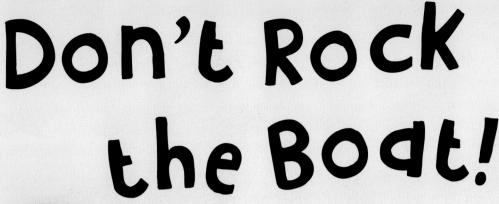

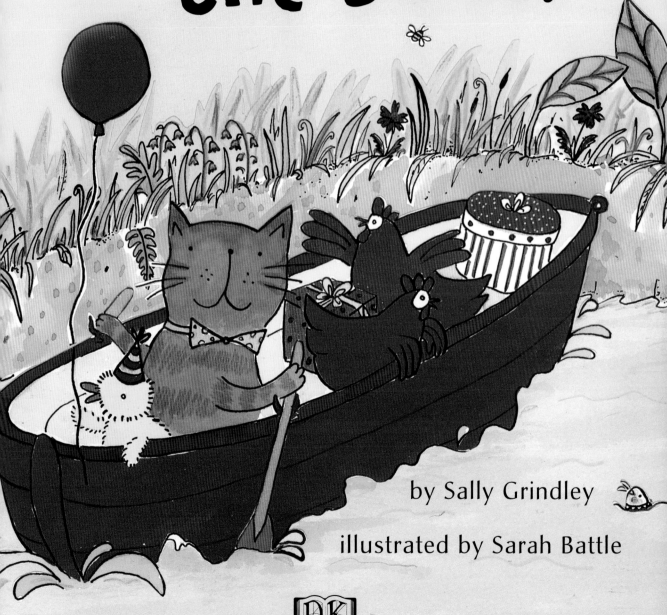

by Sally Grindley

illustrated by Sarah Battle

DK

DK Publishing, Inc.

"What a glorious day for Dottie the Donkey's birthday party!" said Charlie the Cat.
"I'll go there in my boat, but I'll have to be careful not to get wet."

"Can I come with you?" came a voice from the shore.

One fluffy duckling was flapping up and down.

"You can come with me," said Charlie the Cat,
"but whatever you do, **don't rock the boat!**"

The fluffy duckling climbed in oh, so carefully,
and she didn't rock the boat, not a jiggle not a jot.

"Can we come with you?" came voices from the shore. Two happy hens were scooting around and around.

"You can come, too," said Charlie the Cat,
"but whatever you do, **don't rock the boat!**"

The two happy hens climbed in oh, so carefully,
and they only rocked the boat just a jiggle and a jot.

"Can we come with you?"
came voices from the shore.
Three playful puppies were
chasing each other's tails.

"You can come, too," said Charlie the Cat,
"but whatever you do, **don't rock the boat!**"

The three playful puppies
climbed in rather carelessly, and
they rocked the boat with a jostle and a jog.

"Can we come with you?"
came voices from the shore.
Four frisky lambs were
leaping up and down.

"You can come, too," said Charlie the Cat,
"but whatever you do, **don't rock the boat!**"

The four frisky lambs climbed in
very carelessly, and they rocked the
boat with a joggle and a jolt.

"Can we come with you?" came voices from the shore.
Five plump piglets were racing around and around.

"You can come, too," said Charlie the Cat,
"but whatever you do, **don't rock the boat!**"

The five plump piglets jumped in oh, so wildly
that they rocked the boat.
Oh, yes they did! They rocked the boat and . . .

. . . over it went!

"I said, 'Don't rock the boat!'" cried Charlie the Cat.

At last they reached the party with a splish, splash, splosh, and how Dottie the Donkey laughed.

Can you find one duckling, two hens,
three puppies, four lambs, and five piglets?

Hee-haw! Hee-haw!

Activities to Enjoy

If you've enjoyed this story, you might like to try some of these simple, fun activities with your child.

Sink the boat

In the story, the animals overturn their boat. Ask your child to try to sink a toy boat in the bathtub. See how many things you need to put into the boat before it sinks. If you don't have a toy boat, you could use an empty plastic container. Splash the water to rock the boat and see if that makes the boat turn over and sink.

Number frieze

Help your child make a number frieze for the numbers one to five using the animals from the story. Divide a strip of paper into five sections. Ask your child to draw one duckling on the first section, two hens on the next section, three puppies on the next, etc. Then write the correct number on each drawing. Hang up the frieze when it is finished. You could also sing number rhymes to familiarize your child with the numbers one to five. Try "Five Little Monkeys Jumping on the Bed."

Have a party!

Suggest having a pretend birthday party for one of your child's toys. Help her make party hats. Make cone hats or crowns like the ones in the story. Decorate them with glitter, tassels, and colored paper shapes. You could also lay out some food for the party or make pretend food out of empty containers.

Invitations and presents

Choose toys to come to the party. Help your child make invitations for the guests. Wrap empty boxes to make presents. When the party is ready, don't forget to sing "Happy Birthday!"

Dear James
Please come
to a party!
on:
at:
for:

Other Share-a-Story titles to collect:

You're a Big Bear Now, Winston Brown by Paul May,
illustrated by Selina Young

Clara and Buster Go Moondancing by Dyan Sheldon,
illustrated by Caroline Anstey

Where's Bitesize? by Ian Whybrow,
illustrated by Penny Dann

Mama Tiger, Baba Tiger by Juli Mahr,
illustrated by Graham Percy

I Like Me, I Like You by Laurence Anholt,
illustrated by Adriano Gon

Neil's Numberless World by Lucy Coats,
illustrated by Neal Layton

Not Now, Mrs. Wolf! by Shen Roddie,
illustrated by Selina Young

Are You Spring? by Caroline Pitcher,
illustrated by Cliff Wright

The Caterpillar That Roared by Michael Lawrence,
illustrated by Alison Bartlett